2018

FANTAIL BOOKS

£5/6

DETECT-IT-YOURSELF MYSTERIES   Book 2

A gathering of guests at Tudor Close, as featured in the popular Cluedo board-game, gives you the chance to become a super-sleuth. Simply read the stories, spot the clues and then solve the crimes!

There are six absorbing tales of mystery and villainy for you to unravel, each related by one of the well-known Cluedo characters. Miss Scarlett begins the evening with her account of murderous skulduggery aboard a luxury schooner. The Reverend Green turns magician and detective to uncover the culprits behind a summer camp sabotage attempt!

With every story you, the reader, must watch out for the clues that will lead to the unmasking of the villain. To help you, each mystery has its own set of Cluedo notes. All you need is a pencil and your best super-sleuth skills.

So start reading and detect it yourself!

Cluedo®

Detect-It-Yourself Mysteries   Book 2

Joyce McAleer

Illustrated by Bob Wagner

FANTAIL BOOKS

Published by the Penguin Group
Penguin Books Ltd, 27 Wrights Lane, London W8 5TZ, England
Penguin Books USA Inc., 375 Hudson Street, New York, New York 10014, USA
Penguin Books Australia Ltd, Ringwood, Victoria, Australia
Penguin Books Canada Ltd, 10 Alcorn Avenue, Toronto, Ontario, Canada M4V 3B2
Penguin Books (NZ) Ltd, 182–190 Wairau Road, Auckland 10, New Zealand

Penguin Books Ltd, Registered Offices: Harmondsworth, Middlesex, England

First published 1991
3 5 7 9 10 8 6 4

Text copyright © Joyce McAleer, 1991
Illustrations copyright © Bob Wagner, 1991
Cluedo is a registered trademark of Waddington's Games Ltd
Licensed by Copyright Promotions Ltd
All rights reserved

The moral right of the author has been asserted

Filmset in Monophoto 12 on 14 pt Baskerville

Printed in England by Clays Ltd, St Ives plc

Except in the United States of America, this book is sold subject
to the condition that it shall not, by way of trade or otherwise, be lent,
re-sold, hired out, or otherwise circulated without the publisher's
prior consent in any form of binding or cover other than that in
which it is published and without a similar condition including this
condition being imposed on the subsequent purchaser

Dedicated to Cluedo fans everywhere

Contents

How to solve the crimes in Cluedo 2

You can join in the fun by playing detective as you read the six separate crime stories told by your favourite Cluedo characters in this book.

All you have to do is follow the stories carefully, making a mental note – or using pencil and paper, if you wish – whenever you come across anything that sounds suspicious or could be a clue.

Don't forget to look at the pictures too: they may contain vital evidence – or then, again, they may not!

When you arrive at a *CLUEDO NOTES* panel, the time has come to put your powers of detection to the test! Take your time, think logically and, if necessary, look back over the story so far. BUT DON'T TURN THE PAGE UNTIL YOU HAVE EITHER SOLVED THE QUESTION – OR ADMITTED DEFEAT!

Strange Goings-on

Peculiar things were happening in Tudor Close. In the grounds of the elegant mansion, home of the late Dr Black, a fearsome-looking gorilla, dark as the winter-evening sky, crouched behind a low hedge. It watched intently as a maroon Rolls-Royce purred up the driveway and came to a gentle halt outside the front door. From the limousine emerged the figure of an illustrious woman – Cleopatra.

As the chauffeured car drove away, the woman began to mount the stone steps to the entrance. Suddenly the gorilla leapt from its hiding-place with a dreadful roar, and ran after her, beating its chest in true jungle style. Cleopatra shrieked in surprise, then giggled as the primate put a friendly arm round her shoulder and escorted her to the door.

They were ushered inside the house by Buccaneering Blanche, scourge of the Home Counties: a dreadful female pirate, with a sinister eye-patch and a shock of familiar white hair.

'Come in, ye landlubbers!' she cackled, with an

inviting flourish of her cutlass. 'Aharrr, I'd like to see 'e miserable lot walkin' the plank!'

In the Hall they found two other visitors. Robin Hood was warming himself by the large, crackling log fire; Queen Elizabeth I stood haughtily by his side; and a Roman emperor reclined on a *chaise longue*.

'Lovely to see you again, Vivienne!' Robin Hood kissed Cleopatra on the cheek.

The man dressed in Lincoln green was, in fact, Reverend Jonathan Green. He shook the gorilla warmly by the hand. 'Let's see . . . Mrs White is Buccaneering Blanche . . . that's Plum Caesar over there . . . so *you* must be Mustard inside there!'

'Uh, uh!' replied the creature.

'All right,' broke in Mrs Peacock. 'Now that Cleo and her hairy friend have finally arrived, I suggest we go straight into the Dining-Room.'

'What's on the menu?' asked Vivienne Scarlett. 'Ship's biscuits?'

'Aye, with fresh maggots!' cried Buccaneering Blanche.

The guests took their places at the huge dining-table, beautifully set out by Raymond, the butler Mrs White had hired for the occasion. It was a while since they had all seen each other, but now, once again, they had gathered together in Dr Black's memory. On this occasion the inventive Mrs White, who still remained the housekeeper, had requested everyone to come in fancy dress. Dr Black would have been pleased, she thought; he had had a healthy and rather jolly outlook on life.

The diners chatted loudly as they waited for Raymond to bring in the first course. The gorilla never actually spoke, but conversed in a series of expressive grunts and whines.

Professor Peter Plum gathered his ample toga around his body. 'Trust me to choose such a chilly costume on a winter's day,' he complained jovially, placing his slipping laurel wreath back on to the crown of his head. Then, glancing across at Mrs Peacock's shock of bright red locks, he asked, 'Dyed your hair, Mrs P? Oh, sorry – *you're* in costume too!'

'Good evening, all!' Raymond entered and began serving each person with soup.

'Better take off your head, Colonel,' Vivienne said, nudging her hairy neighbour. 'You don't want your whiskers sticking together.'

'Uh, uh!' came the reply.

Everyone watched as the gorilla put its hands up, grasped its head firmly and then deftly pulled it off. There were gasps of shock all round, for they were astounded to see underneath the disguise, not Mike Mustard, but a fresh-faced young man with a wide grin!

'What the –' began Reverend Green.

'Who are *you*?' demanded Mrs White.

'Hold on, I seem to know you,' interrupted Vivienne. 'You're the Colonel's nephew, aren't you?'

'Correct, I am indeed my uncle's nephew!' beamed the young fellow. He stood up and bowed formally. 'Allow me to introduce myself! David Bickerton, from the Laugh-a-lot Novelty Greetings Company. And I have something for *you*, Mrs White!'

The Dining-Room door opened and in came an identical gorilla, bearing a huge bouquet of flowers. It came over to Mrs White and presented her with them. Then it leaned over and gave her a firm hug.

'Lord have mercy!' she exclaimed, lifting her eye-patch. 'What's goin' on?'

'A little present for all your hard work in arranging these dinners,' explained David.

The second gorilla now removed its head – to reveal Colonel Mustard. 'Hello, everyone. Sorry about the little trick. Thought it might amuse you, and it serves to illustrate a little tale of impersonation I have for you later!'

David picked up his own head and started for the door.

'Not stayin'?' asked Mrs White. 'We've plenty o' food.'

'Thanks, but I'm working tonight! Nice to meet

you all. Uncle's told me a lot about you,' he said with a wave. Then he left.

Mike Mustard took his rightful place at the table. 'Hope he hasn't started my soup!'

Mrs White carefully placed her flowers on the floor beside her. She looked tearful, obviously touched by the kind thought.

'Did you each remember to think of a crime story from the past to tell us?' she inquired, dabbing at her eyes with a handkerchief.

Everyone nodded or said yes.

'Shall *I* make a start?' suggested Vivienne cheerfully.

'Yes, go on,' said Reverend Green. 'But it'd better be a good tale. Don't forget I have my bow and arrow here!'

Man Overboard

'My story is rather bizarre,' began Vivienne Scarlett.

'That's what we like to hear!' commented Professor Plum, adjusting his laurel wreath yet again. 'So long as it's true.'

'Oh, it's true all right.'

'And is it a murder?' rasped Mrs White, returning to her piratical voice.

'Listen and you'll find out, you scurvy sea-rover!' retorted Vivienne.

'One Friday morning, a few years back, I was lounging around the house with nothing special to do, when the phone rang. It was Caspar Wolstenholme, a boy who'd lived in one of the cottages on Mummy's estate, where his father ran the stables. Caspar had been my best friend during our early teenage years; we both had a passion for horses and rode everywhere together.

Anyway, Caspar was now no longer a boy. He was a young man – and a rich one, for he was calling me from his luxury schooner moored in the South of France. He invited me to an on-board party he was holding the next day.

"I've arranged for you to pick up a first-class railway ticket at the station," he said.

I thought it was some kind of prank at first. But, sure enough, when I arrived there that afternoon, the ticket was waiting for me!

After a long but luxurious ride through France, followed by a short car drive down to the quay-side, I found myself in a motor-launch on the gorgeous blue waters of the Mediterranean, heading for the most magnificent boat I've ever seen. At anchor was a huge schooner, quite old but ever so elegant, and refurbished to a state of sumptuous luxury. Caspar was out fishing, so I decided to rest until he returned.

The first guests arrived early evening, escorted by Caspar. My, how he had changed since I last saw him. The once awkward and shy boy had become a millionaire entrepreneur. He was muscular and tanned, and wore casual clothes that had obviously cost the earth.

"Vivienne, darling!" he said, embracing me. "You look wonderful. Just like you did down on the farm!"

We talked over old times for a good half-hour, then he took me back out to mingle with the other guests.

"Before I forget, Vivienne, I'll see you on deck, beneath the crow's-nest at the stroke of midnight," he declared mysteriously, leaving me in the company of one Elmer Russell.

Elmer was a tubby businessman, with glasses that made him look like an owl. He was American, very genial, as they usually are.

"I'm Caspar's business adviser," he told me, speaking in short bursts like a machine-gun. "He's a swell guy, y'know. I like his style. No dithering. Takes chances. Made a fortune in buying and selling commodities. Treads on a lot of toes, but keeps strictly legal. Pays me well for my services – I'm on five per cent of everything he makes."

Elmer glanced round sharply as a woman's voice called him.

"Oh, my wife wants me. Lovely meeting you, Vivienne. See you later."

I had obviously caught the eye of a swarthy young chap, who immediately stepped in Elmer's place and introduced himself as Prince Mario. He reckoned he was an impoverished member of the royal family of somewhere I can't remember.

"Caspar's OK, I suppose," he said. "But he's borrowed a lot of money off me over the years . . .

and now that I need it back, he seems to have conveniently forgotten about it!"

After a while I sauntered along the deck to take a look round the boat, and almost had my drink knocked out of my hand by a tall blonde woman who came tearing out of a cabin in great distress.

"What's the matter?" I cried, steadying her.

"A wasp! A wasp! It won't leave me alone!"

I told her it was the drink that the wasp was after and advised her to abandon it on a table. The trick worked and she was instantly wasp-free.

"Ugh! Creepy-crawlies – I hate them!" She was obviously grateful for my assistance. "Thanks. I'm Daisy Prendergast, by the way."

"Ah," I said. "Are you . . . Caspar's girlfriend?"

"Gracious, no!" she giggled. "I *did* go out with him a couple of times once. To be honest, I keep friends with him in the hope that he'll pay Pops the money he owes him. One of his limited companies went to the wall, owing my father thousands and thousands. I do wish Caspar would honour the debt!"

Daisy announced she was going to grab a replacement drink from one of the waiters. Before disappearing, she introduced me to an attractive, middle-aged woman who was sitting alone and staring enigmatically out to sea. She was raven-haired and looked continental. Yet despite her name, Danielle D'Orford, she spoke with an impeccable English accent. She was extremely rich, an heiress to a shipping fortune.

"Do you know Caspar well?" I asked her.

"Sweetie, I was married to him!" she replied with a sad, low laugh.

I was amazed at her story. She had had a whirlwind romance with Caspar, and the marriage had lasted for only a year. She claimed he had used her as a pawn, capitalizing on her connections to make several financially advantageous moves; then he had simply dropped her.

A smooth young man joined us. He had even blonder hair than Daisy Prendergast. He wore tight shiny trousers and a dress-shirt with ruffles down the front.

"Vivienne – meet Claudio Romano," said Danielle. "He's yet another person whom Caspar trampled over on his way to the top."

"Yes, I partnered him in a private zoo venture," nodded Claudio. "We were doing well until Caspar chickened out, leaving me high and dry. Now I'm struggling along as a sort of second-hand crooner with a dance band."

As the night wore on I met everyone on board. The others were all recent acquaintances of Caspar: fellow sailors from the local marina and people he knew only vaguely from the nightclubs on the mainland.

Midnight arrived and I remembered Caspar's request to be under the mast that carried the crow's-nest.

I hadn't realized that he had asked everyone else to be there too! As we gathered on deck in the warm, still night-air, we heard a voice from above. It was Caspar, standing in the little crow's-nest high above our heads.

"My dear, dear friends!" he shouted in a voice that wavered with emotion. "Thank you for coming here to listen to me. All I have to say . . . is that I'm very, very sorry for the . . . the dirty tricks I've played on you . . . on my rise from stable-boy to multi-millionaire."

He paused for a moment, looking down at us all, and then produced a small casket, which we saw him open up.

"All I can say is that I've realized the error of my ways – and I repeat that I'm sincerely sorry . . ."

He stopped abruptly, then suddenly he climbed over the side of the crow's-nest and then jumped, with a cry of anguish, off the side, plummeting down, down into the blue waters below. The casket came crashing down, with white envelopes fluttering from it and landing on the deck around us.

Save for gasps of horror, we remained stunned in silence for a moment. Then we rushed to the side of the boat to try and spot Caspar. There was no sign of him. Claudio dived over the side, followed,

unexpectedly, by Elmer, who pulled off his jacket, shirt and spectacles to follow him into the water.

Danielle went and found the two crew members in their bow-quarters, and they came running to help. One joined the two men in the water, the other fetched a powerful searchlight to comb the scene below.

We continued looking for a full half-hour, then the three exhausted men clambered back on board up a rope-ladder.

"We must inform the coastguards and the police!" announced Elmer grimly.

Shortly afterwards a little police-launch arrived by the schooner and a middle-aged detective clambered aboard with two uniformed officers. He introduced himself as Inspector Gaston Lebrun. After a cursory inspection of the vessel, he called us together.

"No one may leave zee sheep," he declared gravely. "Please wait in zee stateroom. I shall need to question you all individually about Monsieur Wolstenholme's suicide."

He saw me clutching an envelope that had fallen from Caspar's casket.

"What is zat, may I ask?" he inquired.

"It came from Caspar's casket; it fell with him," I explained. "It's a gift. See, it has my name on it. A number of us got one each. Mine contains this short note saying, 'Thanks for the many happy times together on horseback.' And he's enclosed a document giving me his priceless racehorse!"

"Hmm," murmured Lebrun. "And zee others?"

"They've received enormous cheques. Danielle, his ex-wife, got a beautiful diamond tiara. It seems that poor Caspar was making an attempt to pay off past debts before . . . before he jumped."

The guests dispersed but I remained on deck. Lebrun ascended the mast. He was disgruntled to discover that I had followed him up the rope-ladder.

"What are you doing 'ere?" he grunted.

"Helping you look for clues," I puffed, clambering into the little crow's-nest. "I can't believe that Caspar would kill himself. He's not like that. I know because I grew up with him."

"Really?" asked Lebrun. "Then why do you suppose 'e jumped?"

Suddenly I froze in terror and couldn't speak!

Lebrun tutted and repeated his question. I gave my answer by pointing fearfully at the mast just above his head. There, clinging to it, absolutely still, was a monstrous spider! Lebrun's eyes almost popped out of his head; he was even more petrified than I!

"We – we must g-go down as quietly as possible," he whispered in a trembling voice, then ungallantly climbed over the side of the crow's-nest first.

Back on deck he ordered one of his officials to keep watch over the mast, until he could arrange for specialist help in moving the dreaded arachnid.

"Eet is a funnel-web spider, poisonous and indigenous to Australia," he informed me. "I know about zees things. All part of my training, you understand."

"Now we know why Caspar jumped," I said.

"But how did an Australian spider get 'ere?" mused Lebrun.

Then I had a brainwave. "You know, Inspector, I believe this was murder – and I have a theory how the creature came to be in the crow's-nest at the time Caspar was making his announcement!"'

Cluedo' NOTES

Can you guess how the spider got there?

'"It's obvious, Inspector," I continued. "Someone must have planted the spider in Caspar's casket. When he opened it up, he must have almost died of fright and jumped down in sheer panic!"

"Why, yes! But who would want to murder him?" Lebrun rubbed his chin.

"Almost everyone on board! Come into this cabin with me and I'll give you a list . . ."

Lebrun and I sat together, discussing the incident. I told him of my conversations with my fellow guests and described Caspar's last words, as he was about to distribute his generous gifts in order to make amends for his allegedly cheap-skate behaviour.

"If I'm not putting my foot into hot water," asked Lebrun, "may I ask why Monsieur Wolstenholme gave you a racehorse? What was he recompensing you for?"

"Nothing – except for fond memories of our youth!" I replied. "That's why you have no need to suspect me! I was delighted to meet Caspar again. I haven't seen him since he was about fifteen."

"So you think zee people I should consider for questioning are ziss Prince Mario, Danielle d'Orford, Claudio Romano, Elmer Russell and –"

"And Daisy Prendergast," I said. "The rest of the guests on board are only on nodding terms with him, and the crew are new, as he's only just taken delivery of it."

"Whom do you suggest I commence with?"

I thought hard for a moment and then realized I could narrow the field of suspects down to three . . .'

Cluedo' NOTES

Which two of these guests has Vivienne Scarlett eliminated from her inquiries – and why? You may have to look back through the story to jog your memory!

Daisy Prendergast

Prince Mario

Elmer Russell

Danielle d'Orford

Claudio Romano

"You can forget Daisy Prendergast," I explained to Lebrun. "She went to pieces when a wasp chased her. So I hardly think she'd have the stomach to plant a spider in Caspar's casket!"

"Aha, very observant of you. And pray tell me, who is zee other person we can forget?"

"Elmer Russell, who did very well advising Caspar on financial matters. He told me he received five per cent of the profits."

With Lebrun, I went back to the stateroom, where the guests were still waiting. The buzz of excited conversation stopped as we entered.

"Any news of Caspar?" queried Daisy, her eyes red with crying.

"I'm afraid not," answered Lebrun. "My men are looking – and zee coastguards are searching too. I'll let you know when there is news."

He then asked Prince Mario, Danielle and Claudio to come and join us on deck. We all stopped at the mast beneath the crow's-nest.

"Does anyone recall anything that may help with my investigation?" asked the Inspector.

"Like what?" snapped Prince Mario. "This is a straightforward suicide, isn't it?"

"It could be – and then again, maybe not."

"What do you mean by that?" Claudio Romano looked shocked.

"I mean what I say," said Lebrun, watching for

any tell-tale reactions on the faces of our suspects. "Eet is my duty to consider all possibilities."

"Shouldn't you be helping to look for Caspar?" Danielle asked the officer on watch at the bottom of the mast. "What are you standing on guard for?"

"I – er – I'm keeping my eye on the b-big poisonous spider up there," he stuttered.

"What?" spluttered Danielle.

"It's true. There is a spider up there," intervened Lebrun. "I believe it may have been the cause of Monsieur Wolstenholme falling to his – falling into the sea."

The Inspector pointed to the vacant cabin in which I had talked to him earlier. "Would you all be so kind as to take a seat in there whilst I speak to my men? You, too, Miss Scarlett, please."

Prince Mario, Danielle and Claudio did as they were asked. As I followed them inside, Lebrun whispered to me briefly.

"You are my – my ferret!" He winked at me.

"I think you mean I'm your mole!" I corrected him with a smile.

We took our seats in the opulently furnished cabin. It was a curious feeling for me to sit there, knowing that, if my suspicions were correct, one of us was a murderer.

"Why does this detective need to interrogate us?" sighed Prince Mario. "It's been a horrible evening.

He should let us go home."

"I quite agree with you," declared Danielle. "He has no right to keep us on board with a funnel-web spider at large! For all we know, it could be creeping around in here right now!"

She gathered her gown and curled her legs up beside her on the bench seat.

I shuddered at what she'd said. After all, I'd seen the beast at close quarters!

"I believe we're suspected of murder," said Claudio in a quiet voice. "I'll bet you the Inspector comes in accusing us!"

The door of the cabin opened and in strode Lebrun. He sat with us and took out a little notebook and pencil.

"I'll come straight to the bush; I won't beat about it," he announced. "I may be investigating a case of – murder!"

"Told you so," smiled Claudio.

"Murder by *spider*?" cried Prince Mario. "Are you serious?"

"There have been many such ingenious methods in zee annals of crime," continued Lebrun, licking his pencil and preparing to take notes. "Now, which of you had access to such a funnel-web spider?"

"Funnel-web spiders come from Australia," added Prince Mario. "You forget you are on an ocean-going vessel. This ship has probably been to Australia. A spider could easily have climbed aboard there."

"Not this sheep!" retorted Lebrun. "I have just checked with zee crew. It has never left these shores for years."

"Oh, don't make such a complete fool of yourself, Inspector!" scoffed Danielle.

Until this point I had remained silent. But I decided to speak up – for I now had some firm evidence which confirmed someone's guilt. Lebrun's idea to send me into the cabin as a mole had proved effective!'

Cluedo' NOTES

Who's guilty – and why?

'"I don't think the Inspector *is* making a fool of himself!" I told Danielle. "You know more about this business than you're letting on."

"And what precisely do you mean by that?!" she hissed.

"When we first came into this cabin, you complained that Monsieur Lebrun had no right to keep us on board with a funnel-web spider at large."

"So?"

"The officer on guard told us it was a big poisonous spider. How could you have known what type it was – unless you were the person who brought it here?"

"Rubbish!" Danielle went red with rage and pointed to Claudio. "He's your man. He has contacts in the zoological trade. At one time he ran a small zoo with Caspar."

"Huh! I only got it for *you!*" snarled Claudio.

"Shut up, you idiot!"

Inspector Lebrun stood up. "Well," he said, "I believe that wraps up zee case!"'

'So they were in league, then, this Danielle and Claudio?' asked Mustard.

'Yes,' confirmed Vivienne. 'They'd formed an attachment for one another and had decided to take revenge upon Caspar. Claudio had stolen the spider from the zoo of one of

his friends, and Danielle had brought it on board and hidden it in the casket in Caspar's quarters. I doubt she realized it would be opened in such public circumstances.'

'What a clever plan!' exclaimed Plum. 'Worthy of a devious Roman emperor!'

'But not, I suspect, half so devious as Caspar Wolstenholme,' announced Vivienne mysteriously.

'How d'you mean?' inquired Mrs White.

'Because I'm sure I've seen him since! Only last year I was travelling on the London Underground. The train had started up at Green Park and just before we disappeared into the tunnel, I caught sight of a shabby tramp on the platform. It was Caspar, I'll swear to it!'

The dinner guests sighed in amazement.

'Goodness knows what he's up to – but I believe it's not the last time our paths will cross!' continued Vivienne.

She stretched out a long leg under the table and brushed her toe against Plum's foot. He look puzzled.

'That reminds me,' said Vivienne, faking a look of alarm. 'My poisonous asp seems to have disappeared. Anyone seen it?'

Plum gave a yell and jumped back in shock. 'It's got my –'

He stopped in mid-sentence when he spotted Vivienne's grinning face, then blushed and sat down again.

The Brain of Brickhampton

'Right, we'll return to my schooldays for the next story,' announced Professor Peter Plum.

'Ah, an ancient history lesson?' sniggered Reverend Green.

'Not quite so ancient as your childhood reminiscences would be,' retorted Plum.

''Ere, mind if we get on with it?' demanded Mrs White.

'OK, I'm taking you back more years than I care to remember. Back to Brickhampton Town Hall on a warm July evening. The place is packed to bursting with parents, grandparents and children, because this is the finals of the Inter-County Schools Quiz!

Up on the stage sit two teams of schoolkids, locked in deadly combat: rivals for the coveted gold cup, which will bring their school untold honour for the

forthcoming year. On one side is North Wigdale High, represented by a nondescript trio of ruffians, whose names escape me; and on the other, the glorious Brickhampton School team, consisting of Teddy Bingham, George Boardman and their captain – none other than me, Peter Plum!

These two finalist schools are neck and neck, and it's time for the last question, which will decide the winner.

"Ready, schools?" asks Mr Bannister, the doddery question-master, a retired headmaster with a permanently sour expression. "Tell me, please – how high is Mount Everest?"

Bzzzz! Young George Boardman hits his buzzer. Thank goodness he's on our team! Teddy and I know the answer, but as usual it's George who gets in first.

"Yes, Boardman?" asks Mr Bannister.

"Er – um – let me see, now," stutters George. "It's – um –"

"Yes? I must have an answer . . ."

"Oh, it's on the tip of my tongue. It's . . . wait a minute . . ., ah, yes, its 29,028 feet!"

Mr Bannister looks astounded by the accuracy of George's answer, then he nods. "You are correct. Congratulations! I declare Brickhampton School the winners of the competition for this year!"

The applause is tumultuous as I step forward to

receive the cup for the school, and George, at my side, accepts the special prize for answering the most questions of the evening.

Now, all that happened the year before my story proper.

The following year, Teddy and I were walking to school on the day of the Inter-County Schools Quiz Final. Tonight, after a number of exhausting knock-out rounds, was to be the big event! Once again, Teddy, George and I had been selected to represent the school.

"Remember what George Boardman won last year? A massive train-set!" exclaimed Teddy enviously.

"I know. Makes you sick," I replied. "I'm glad he helped us win but I can't understand how he answers correctly all the time. Without exception he presses the buzzer, then mumbles and falters before finally spluttering out the right answer. It's as if he were waiting for divine inspiration!"

"Yes, he's such a complete duffer in class," observed Teddy. "Why, he couldn't even spell 'veterinary' in yesterday's English test!"

We looked sheepishly at one another, then exploded into giggles as it dawned on us that neither could we!

First lesson that morning was History, one of our least favourite subjects. Medieval Maddocks was droning on and on about the House of Hanover.

"Nervous about tonight?" I whispered to Teddy, who was sitting next to me.

"A bit," he replied with a grin. "Though we don't need to be – with brainbox George on the team!"

Suddenly I felt a sharp series of taps on my head. George from behind, was tapping out a message in Morse code on my skull.

"Know what that means?" he hissed, when he'd finished.

"No, do tell me!"

"It means 'pay attention to Mr Maddocks!' Good, eh?"

"I know you're good at Morse code but you don't have to give us a demonstration at every possible opportunity," complained Teddy.

"It's the *only* thing he's good at!" I added cruelly.

"We'll see who comes out tops tonight!" smirked George.

Medieval Maddocks's voice boomed out. "Boardman, are you talking in class? Pay attention, boy! Who was the first British monarch from the House of Hanover?"

"Er – was it – um," struggled George. He gave what he thought was a serious reply. "Was it – um – the Queen of Hearts?"

Everyone collapsed in fits of laughter.

"Bah! If it weren't for the competition tonight," growled Maddocks, "I'd give you a detention. George I, boy! You of all people should know that!"'

'Evening came, and Teddy and I strolled, with our mothers and fathers, along Brickhampton High Street towards the Town Hall. We had both been scrubbed until our cheeks shone and we were wearing our best blazers. George wasn't with us: he was being taken by his doting parents in their car, pulling an ancient caravan.

Teddy and I lingered outside the Town Hall for a while to take the air, whilst our mothers and fathers went inside to get good seats. We stood on the corner in the sunshine, and watched as the Boardmans drew up. Mr and Mrs Boardman alighted from the car, followed by George and his Uncle Gilbert, an eccentric figure for those days. He had long, straggly grey hair and invariably wore a flamboyant bow-tie.

"George isn't in the least like his uncle," laughed Teddy. "Uncle Gilbert's reckoned to be a genius. Mustn't run in the family, that's all I can say!"

Mrs Boardman, dressed up to the nines, smoothed down George's hair and led him proudly past us and into the building.

"See you inside, boys," smiled George confidently.

He prodded me in the tummy. "Bzzzz! Fingers ready?"

We nodded amiably and continued to watch George's father and uncle. Evidently they were not going to watch the contest, but disappeared instead into the caravan and settled on the seats.

"Funny, isn't it?" said Teddy.

"What is?"

"The way George's family fusses round him – yet those two can't be bothered to go inside to see the quiz."

"Oh, they always do that. Haven't you noticed? I always thought it was odd that they wait outside. Perhaps they can't stand the tension!"

We strolled up to the caravan and peered in through the window. Over a stove George's father was pouring hot water from a kettle into a tiny teapot, whilst Uncle Gilbert poured milk into cups. Alongside them on the table lay an antiquated radio full of dials and knobs and switches, and beside that was a pile of quick-reference books and en-cyclopaedias.

"Huh!" whispered Teddy. "George must have been swotting on the way here!"

Mr Boardman looked up and caught sight of us. He gave us a sneer and shooed us away with a hand. Then he pulled down all the little blinds.

"Miserable ol' meanie!" muttered Teddy. "Who

wants to spy on his scrap-heap anyway? Look at the crackpot aerial on the roof!"

"Yes. He's an amateur radio enthusiast. Clever stuff, really. Makes all his own equipment and speaks to people all over the world, according to George."

"Perhaps he receives messages from the moon!"

"No doubt he will," I replied seriously, "in a few short years."

It was then that I guessed why George's father and uncle were going to hang around in their caravan instead of going into the Town Hall!'

Cluedo' NOTES

Can you work out why Mr Boardman and Uncle Gilbert remain in their curiously equipped caravan?

' "Why are you staring into space?" asked Teddy.

"Sorry, I was thinking . . . I know how George gets everything right in the quiz!"

"How?"

"He receives messages by radio from these two in the caravan! Between them, they probably know most of the answers. And anything they don't know, they look up quickly in those books!"

"Yeah!" breathed Teddy. "But hold on. George doesn't wear headphones or anything. You can see his ears as clearly as anything 'cos his hair's cut short like a scrubbing-brush."

"Hmmm, you're right. Maybe I'm accusing him unjustly. All the same, it's a good theory!"

Time was pressing on, so we entered the Town Hall to prepare for our forthcoming ordeal. As it was a hot night we went along to the wash-room at the back of the stage to splash cold water on our faces. Inside we discovered George, his shirt sleeves rolled up, drying his face. We hung our blazers next to his and headed for the wash-basin.

George finished with the roller-towel, grabbed the blazer nearest to him and set off for the stage.

"You'll be late," he grinned. "I'll just have to manage without you!"

Teddy and I dried our faces and put on our blazers – or so we thought! Mine felt decidedly lop-sided, so I delved into the inside pocket. I pulled out a small, heavy metal box with an on/off switch and what looked like a small microphone.

"Whoops!" I exclaimed. "I've taken the wrong blazer. This must be George's!"

Teddy and I stared at the instrument. I switched it on and a little rod popped out and poked me.

"What is it?" asked Teddy. "A two-way radio, like you suspected?"

"It's a radio of some sort . . . no speaker . . . just a microphone."

"But what does this little rod do?" demanded Teddy.

"I've no idea!" I said. "But it must poke him in the ribs a lot!"

But then I did know! I understood precisely how this ingenious little gadget made George Boardman appear to be so clever!'

Cluedo NOTES

Well, how does the electronic box of tricks give George all the answers?

' "It's like I said. This *is* how George gets everything right!" I explained. "The microphone relays the questions from the quiz to Mr Boardman and Uncle Gilbert outside. Then they transmit the answers to George."

"Yes, I gathered that – but it still doesn't explain how George receives the messages. No headphones, remember."

"He doesn't need any!" I declared. "He doesn't *hear* anything!"

Teddy was utterly confused.

"It's so simple – and clever!" I continued. "George's dad taps out the answers in Morse code. George gets little prods in the ribs from the little rod instead of bleeps!"

"Wow, yeah! I think you've got it!" whistled Teddy. "That's why he's slow in answering. He's actually decoding the message!"

"Exactly!"

Footsteps clattered towards the wash-room.

"Quick! That'll be George coming back!" hissed Teddy.

I replaced the radio receiver, whipped off the blazer and replaced it on the wall-hook.

"Sorry, you two," announced George, looking relieved to see Teddy and I were still in our shirt-sleeves. "Silly me, I took the wrong blazer!"

He grabbed his own and tossed my blazer carelessly towards me. Then he scurried back out of the wash-room.

"What a swizzler!" exclaimed Teddy. "Imagine the shame for Brickhampton School if this got out!"

"It doesn't need to!" I cried."I'm going to give Boardman Senior and Uncle Gilbert a piece of my mind! C'mon, we've just got time."

We raced outside, past the bewildered commissionaire and into the street. The caravan was occupied and the door was half-open. We peered inside cautiously and discovered a treasure-house of reference books, maps and charts. The radio transmitter was switched on, with little lights glowing. From the loudspeaker we could hear muffled sounds which obviously were coming from within the Town Hall via George's pocket radio. "We'll beat you hollow!" George's voice cackled shrilly. He was obviously baiting one of the competitors onstage!

"Shall I remove a valve from the set?" suggested Teddy.

"Better not – you'll probably electrocute yourself," I advised him.

At that moment I saw Teddy's elder brother Tom, on a week's leave from his army unit, sauntering towards the Hall. He was coming to watch Teddy in action.

"I have a much better idea!" I smiled, beckoning Tom to come over to us.

"Hello, boys. Shouldn't you be in the Town Hall by now?" he asked pleasantly.

"We will be in a tick," I said. "But will you do us a big favour – and bring a rotter his just desserts?"

"What?"

"Jump inside the van, Tom, and close the door behind you. Don't let anyone in – no matter how much they rant and rave. OK?"

"Er – if you say so," murmured Tom uncertainly.

"Being in the army, you know Morse code, don't you?"

"I should say so!"

"Good. Now listen for the questions that come through the loudspeaker and tap out a gob-bledygook answer for each one. Any sort of tripe will do. But whatever you do, don't give the *right* answer, OK?"

Poor Tom didn't have time to answer before I slammed the door on him and retired to the pavement. We were just in time, for George's father and Uncle Gilbert appeared from round the corner, the latter carrying a bag of sugar.

"I told you to pack sugar," moaned Uncle Gilbert. "I can't stand tea without!"

"Hurry up and get in the caravan!" snapped Mr Boardman. "The competition must be about to start!"

What a shock they had when they discovered that

the caravan's door was locked. They pulled and twisted the handle to no avail. They couldn't see Tom inside because the blinds were down.

"You fool! You've managed to lock us out!" stormed Mr Boardman. "And I left the keys inside!"

"B-but . . ."

"Never mind the excuses! We'll have to run home and get the spare key! It'll take us nearly half an hour. At least we might catch the end of the contest!"

The two men set off at a trot down the road.

The commissionaire poked his head round the Town Hall door. "'Ere you two, you're on now!"

We charged back inside and on to the stage, where George was already seated. The opposition were there too, waiting nervously.

The auditorium lights dimmed and the curtains opened to polite applause from the waiting audience.

The clapping continued as crusty old Mr Bannister came on stage and introduced the proceedings. He then sat down gravely on his small dais and produced a large envelope from his inside pocket. Ripping it open, he took out a sheaf of papers.

"I have here the questions for this year's final of the Inter-County Schools Quiz. We shall now begin."

A hush fell over the auditorium.

"Question one," began Mr Bannister. "Who is the patron saint of Scotland?"

Bzzzz! Predictably it was George Boardman that hit the button first. Teddy and I grinned at one another.

"Yes, Boardman?"

"It is – um –" began George in his customary manner. "It is – St Haggis."

Screams of laughter came from the audience, and George went bright red.

"I'm afraid not," replied old Bannister, his mouth almost curling up into a smile. "It's St Andrew."

We waited until the peals of laughter had died down.

"Next question. Who was the first American President?"

Bzzz! Young George pressed again. Teddy and I, although we knew the answer, were quite content to allow him to go ahead.

"Let me think . . . now, it must have been . . ." procrastinated George, as the clever little radio device in his pocket tapped out the answer. "Yes, it was – Wild Bill Hickok!"

More screams of laughter followed. Mr Bannister gave George a long, hard stare.

"No, boy. It was George Washington."

George's face began to crumble.

"Question three," continued Mr Bannister, "and

if I receive any more facetious or disruptive responses from you, Master Boardman, I shall have no alternative but to ask you to leave the stage. Now, what is the main diet of the African elephant?"

This question stumped us. Not even George buzzed straight away, but the determined prodding in his ribs was too much for him. Bzzzz!

"Yes, Boardman?"

"Er – is it – um – whatever gets in its way?"

This time George's ludicrous reply brought the house down. The audience rolled in their seats, convulsing in laughter. I felt genuinely sorry for poor George, wondering if my revenge was perhaps too harsh.

Mr Bannister stood up and simply pointed to the side of the stage. "Off, buffoon! Your team-mates will have to continue without you!"

Without a word, the red-faced George vacated his seat and disappeared into the wings . . .'

Cluedo NOTES

As a detective you should retain every scrap of information you come across, however trivial it may seem! Let's see if you can answer these three questions before looking back through the story. Don't worry – it's not the Inter-County Schools Quiz!

1. *How high is Mount Everest?*
2. *Who was the first British Monarch belonging to the House of Hanover?*
3. *What is the registration of the Boardmans' car?*

'And what happened after that?' asked Mrs Peacock.

'Oh, Teddy and I won the quiz, of course,' chuckled Plum. 'And I took the special prize – a pair of binoculars.'

'No, I mean what happened to George?' insisted Mrs Peacock.

'Well, I wasn't there to see, but Tom gave us a good report! Upon hearing the hoo-hah over the radio, he slipped out of the caravan and stood nonchalantly on the street-corner to watch the fun. Apparently Mrs Boardman dragged young George by one ear, out of the Town Hall and almost threw him into the caravan. Minutes later Mr Boardman and Uncle Gilbert jogged up with the spare key, only to be greeted by Mrs B. with ear-splitting screams and blows about the head from a heavy volume of an encyclopaedia!'

'I feel sorry for George,' sighed Vivienne.

'No need. The experience was good for him,' reported Plum. 'He was ribbed for a few days at school but then he actually started to study and became quite a clever fellow eventually.'

'I wonder where he is now,' mused Reverend Green.

Plum coughed and then prevaricated like George Boardman. 'Er – um – well, I believe he went into the Church . . .'

A Packet of Sparklers

'Me next?' ventured Elizabeth Peacock, waving a regal finger in the air.

'I don't think anyone's going to dare disagree with Elizabeth I,' said Vivienne.

'How gracious of you all! Now, my little story brings back painful memories, but thanks to my determined efforts, everything turned out wonderfully well in the end.' Mrs Peacock smiled and fingered her exquisite diamond necklace. 'You'll remember my daughter Antonia's eighteenth birthday party?'

The other guests nodded, recalling the lavish event with pleasure.

'Well, whilst you were all enjoying yourselves, a desperate drama was unfolding . . .'

'I naturally had to look my best for the occasion, so I went along to Formby & Metcalfe, which, as you all know, is an exclusive West End store. Mr Metcalfe himself showed me such a magnificent diamond necklace, I just had to buy it there and then. It's the one I'm wearing now. Very beautiful – and very expensive!

Foolishly, I rushed around so much preparing for the party that I didn't manage to insure the jewels straight away. Very remiss of me – and it nearly cost me dearly!

Anyway, to get back to what happened on that fateful evening: the party, you'll recall, was held at the Royal Crown Hotel, where I took a suite for the weekend. Many other guests booked rooms too. After all, it was to be a big affair. Family and friends from far and wide were invited; some from abroad even. Antonia, who was away at college, was due to arrive shortly before the party and share my suite for the rest of our stay.

When I booked in on the day before the party, I took the precaution of having the manager, James, put my jewels in the hotel's safe. The following night Antonia arrived with her luggage. I asked the manager to retrieve my necklace from the safe. He gave his key – the only key, he informed me – to his assistant manager, who brought my jewels promptly to me. I put them into Antonia's vanity-case and asked Alan, the porter, to take all her luggage up to our suite. Then Antonia joined some of her young friends in the lounge and started to introduce them to me. Alan had already gone up with the luggage.

I followed him a few minutes later. But what a calamity! My foolishness again, I'm afraid. I entered our suite to find Alan on the floor, hastily reassembling the contents of the vanity-case.

"So sorry, madam," he mumbled, with a face as red as a beetroot. "This case wasn't locked properly and everything spilled out."

I assured him it was all right and not to worry. Then I remembered my necklace. It'd been in that case – and was nowhere to be seen! In panic, I looked around.

"I – I've not seen it, madam," blubbered Alan over and over again, slumping down into a chair as if in a state of shock.

Finally I found it, still in the case, which was beneath the chair where Alan was now sitting. I was cross, I can tell you. But I told Alan to forget the matter and bade him goodbye. He said that he was going off duty, which was a relief. Such incompetence I could do without on an important occasion!

Never mind – a short nap would refresh me! Then it would be time to put on my gorgeous new gown and jewels. I relaxed in the bedroom and really began to look forward to the birthday celebrations.

Then I heard someone enter the suite. I assumed it was Antonia.

"Hello, darling," I called. No reply came, but as the walls were very solid I presumed she hadn't heard my greeting.

Shortly afterwards, when I was up and about, I was surprised to see Antonia burst in excitedly, calling, "Oh, Mummy, people kept me talking downstairs. I'll have to hurry and get ready!"

"But didn't you come in a few moments ago?"

Antonia replied that she hadn't.

"Somebody did," I told her.

"Probably that little red-haired maid," said Antonia. "I bumped into her as I came out of the lift."
The party was soon in full swing, and it was wonderful! Oh, but of course, you all know – because you were there! Lady Mulberry was as tiresome as ever, going on and on about the last party she held at her country home.

However, she did make a great fuss of Antonia and complimented me on the success of the party. She gave my necklace an admiring glance too. I was pleased because I know she's a real expert on diamonds. I told her where I'd bought them.

"Good choice of jeweller," she said. "I often buy from there. The staff are so helpful. Last year Sam did an excellent job of mending my gold watch. Pity he's no longer there."

Antonia was thrilled with all her lovely cards and presents. The food was delicious, the music delightful . . . it was all simply heavenly. Until I met Oliver, that is. I was trying to make my way through the lively throng of youthful dancers to get myself a cocktail.

"Sit down, Mrs Peacock. I'll fetch you a glass," said a kind voice from just behind me.

It was Oliver Kingston, the father of one of Antonia's friends. He's a widower; a very sweet gentleman. As we sat and talked I couldn't help noticing that he was staring intently at my neck.

"Excuse me, but may I take a closer look at your necklace?" he asked.

"Of course," I answered. Mr Kingston was obviously impressed by my good taste – or so I thought!

However, the expression on his face as he ran his fingers over the necklace made me feel apprehensive. Were the diamonds of inferior quality? Was he going to ask me how much I'd paid for them and then tell me that I should have haggled for a lower price? When Mr Kingston finally did speak, the reality was far worse than any of these alternatives.

He said simply, "My dear Mrs Peacock, do you realize that these diamonds are fake?"

"Nonsense!" I spluttered, feeling my face redden with embarrassment. "You must be mistaken. I bought this necklace only yesterday. I have the receipt from Formby & Metcalfe here in my handbag."

"I'm so utterly sorry, Mrs Peacock," said Mr Kingston. "But I've been in this business for many, many years and I have an eye for ... what doesn't seem quite right. I couldn't believe that a person of your taste would wear fake jewellery for such an important family occasion. That's why I asked to examine the necklace. Please believe me, I am not mistaken. I cannot offer you any explanation; Formby & Metcalfe are jewellers of the highest repute. I simply cannot believe that they have sold you those stones as genuine, even though they are expertly crafted."

I sat there stunned and bewildered. Mr Kingston, obviously feeling very awkward, joined the other guests, and after a few minutes I did the same.

No one guessed that, beneath my cheerful chatter and smiles, I was in turmoil. I had no doubt that Mr Kingston was right. So what had happened? I considered the possibilities. Had Formby & Metcalfe sold me fake jewels deliberately? According to Mr Kingston, that was hardly possible. Anyway, Mr Metcalfe was virtually an institution in the jewellery trade and would never have risked his business reputation by being dishonest. So what was left? The jewels must have been switched – my real ones stolen and substituted with fakes. That was my obvious and only conclusion. But it, too, was incredible. The necklace had been in my possession until I'd handed them over to the hotel manager to be put into the safe.

If such a thing *had* happened, then someone in the hotel was responsible. But who? And how could that person have had a copy of the necklace? A copy exact and perfect in every detail. I'd shown the jewellery to no one before arriving at the hotel; there hadn't been time. Oh, no, I groaned, remembering I hadn't had time to insure them. At that moment I determined to somehow find my jewels – my real jewels. Yet, in order not to spoil Antonia's party, my inquiries had to be discreet.

I looked over to James the hotel manager, briskly issuing orders to his staff. "Bring more chocolate gateaux, Ann," he called to a waitress. "There's a guest with luggage over by the lift, Joe," he told the porter who'd taken over from the clumsy Alan.

He turned to his assistant manager, a surly-looking fellow, and smiled with satisfaction. "Things are going great tonight, Sam," he grinned.

I didn't like the way James grinned. He was smug and knowing. Too knowing? Was James the thief? I had no proof, no evidence, nothing. My investigations would have to be carried out in a thorough, objective fashion – just like a real detective's – because, of course, the last thing I wanted to do was to call in the police. It would be such a spectacle. Questions would be asked; innocent people upset. Antonia, so happy and radiant tonight, would be devastated.

No, it was up to *me* to sort out this unhappy matter. And, in a way, I must admit that, despite my initial shock and anger, I was curious and intrigued. My dear friends, you all know how I love a good mystery – and here I had a real-life one on my hands. I actually began to relish the thought of solving it!

In as casual a manner as I could muster, I strolled over to the reception-desk.

"Congratulations on your organizational skills," I remarked to James. "Things are certainly going well!"

"Yes, everyone seems to be having an excellent time," he beamed.

"Thanks to you and your staff. You must hand pick them."

"Well, we do take great care. Some of our staff members have been with us for years and our trainees learn everything there is to know about the hotel business. We want only the best for Royal Crown guests!"

"You take on experienced people too?"

"Oh, yes, as long as they come highly recommended," he answered. "If they've worked in other top-class establishments, for instance. I can't divulge personal details, you understand, but suffice to say that Sam, my assistant manager, was even in the employ of a member of the aristocracy – a titled lady!"

"I'm impressed!" I said, my attention caught by the glint of the bright red hair of the chambermaid as she hurried up the sweeping staircase.

Quickly I made my way through the crowded room and caught the lift to the first floor. The lift doors opened just in time for me to meet the said maid, as she reached the top of the stairs.

"Oh, hello," I called, as if in pleasant surprise. "I should have taken the stairs too. They say it's a good way to keep fit."

"Good evenin', madam," answered the maid breathlessly.

She had a cautious, crafty look in her eyes, and her voice had a harsh and slightly hostile edge. "I can't be bothered waitin' for the lift sometimes, specially when we've got a party on. It's quicker to use the stairs."

I'll have to tread carefully, I thought, if I'm to get anything from this quarter. I could see by the badge she was wearing that her name was Maggie.

"What a pretty name!" I ventured.

"Short for Margaret but I prefer Maggie," she muttered.

"So do I!" I answered, my mind working overtime to pick up any clue. "By the way, I was resting when you came into my suite earlier. Did you need to ask me anything?"

"What, madam?" Her face was now as red as her hair! "I didn't go into your suite."

"Oh, that's strange," I said. "I heard someone come in, and my daughter saw you moments later."

"Oh, yes!" Her face brightened. "You're right, I did. I put some fresh flowers on your dressing-table."

"Did you come only to my suite?" I asked this

because it had just occurred to me that, in order for Maggie to be catching the lift so soon, she couldn't have had time to enter any other rooms.

"No, I'd already changed their flowers, but . . ." Her face went even redder, her manner more flustered. My hopes rose. Had I solved the puzzle so soon?

"Well, it's a bit 'ard to explain, madam," she said. "You see, I did go to your room at the same time as all the others but you were . . . busy."

"Busy?"

"Tellin' Alan off. I could 'ear you through the door. I didn't like to come in. I thought – well, to tell the truth, I thought 'e was up to 'is old tricks."

"Tricks? What tricks?" I inquired calmly, concealing my excitement.

"I don't like gossiping about another worker, madam," Maggie went on, now eager to do exactly that! "But 'e's been warned a good few times about pinchin' towels an' soap an' stuff from guests' rooms. 'E used to pinch from the 'otel store, but the new stock-control clerk is keen as mustard, so now 'e takes from the guests. There's no way of knowin', except when guests complain. I think 'e gives the stuff to 'is family as presents. I've even 'eard that 'e sells it round the pubs in the village. 'Ow daft can you get, madam? I ask you! 'Is days 'ere are numbered, that's for sure!"

When she'd gone, I took my mini-notepad from my bag and jotted down the possible suspects – the only people I'd come into contact with since I'd purchased the necklace. From this list I was then able to eliminate the three most unlikely perpetrators of the crime, leaving me with four names to investigate.'

Cluedo NOTES

These are Mrs Peacock's seven suspects. Which three do you think she can safely eliminate?

1. Mr Metcalfe of Formby & Metcalfe
2. James, the hotel manager
3. Sam, the assistant manager
4. Alan, the porter
5. Maggie, the chambermaid
6. Lady Mulberry, a guest
7. Oliver Kingston, a guest

'I crossed out Mr Metcalfe, because he would never risk his reputation or his established jewellery business; Maggie, because her excuse was quite plausible enough; and Oliver Kingston, because if he were guilty, why on earth would he have identified the necklace as a fake!

Realizing I might be missed downstairs, I rejoined the party.

"Ah, there you are, Mummy!" called Antonia. "Isn't it *the* most wonderful, *the* most brilliant party in the universe?"

"Yes, sweetheart," I agreed, helping myself to a cocktail. At least, it would be if I could get to the bottom of this mystery, I thought.

"Antonia," I said, "do you *like* my necklace? Take a close look at it."

She cast a puzzled glance at me. "It's beautiful, Mummy. Really it is."

"But can you tell if it's real?"

"Of course I can," laughed Antonia. "Mummy, you are a scream! Oh, look – Peter and Jenny are waving me over. See you later!"

And off she went, leaving me to my thoughts, which were soon to be interrupted by the booming voice of Lady Mulberry.

"My dear, I'm having such a lovely, lovely time!" As always, I felt instantly overshadowed by her large bulk and overpowering manner. I watched her take

a lace handkerchief from her otherwise empty evening bag and blow her nose noisily.

"So glad you're enjoying it, Lady Mulberry," I said. "It does seem to be a success."

"It certainly is!" she replied, gazing at my necklace. "My, my, that is a pretty piece. Formby & Metcalfe, you said?"

"That's right," I answered. "You . . . you don't think it looks cheap, do you?"

"Cheap?" Why, anyone can see at a glance that it must have cost a small fortune!" she thundered, fondling my necklace with a chubby hand encased in exquisite gold rings, and a jewelled watch on her wrist. She squinted closely at it. "Simply magnificent, my dear!"

During the next few minutes I formulated a plan. The party was going so well that I wouldn't be missed for the short time it would take me to put it into action. The first step was to see James the manager.

"Excuse me," I said, "but may I have my daughter's jewellery box from the safe? I'd like to show a particular ring to another guest. It's quite all right – Antonia won't mind. She's over there."

As I expected, James looked puzzled. "But your daughter hasn't anything in the safe, Mrs Peacock!"

"Are you sure?" I asked, feigning surprise.

"Quite sure," he insisted. "In fact the safe is empty."

"Please be a dear and take another look for me," I implored.

James shrugged and turned into the office at the back of the reception area. I followed, twittering about how I was sure the jewellery box was there. I knew I was making James feel awkward, but I had to see for myself. He opened the safe. It was quite empty.

"I hope your daughter's not lost her jewellery box," said James, a concerned expression clouding his face.

I assured him he was not to worry. Now I knew my jewels had not been placed in the safe by anyone – so they must be elsewhere! Next step was to find Maggie the maid. It didn't take long. I strolled down a passage of offices marked "Private", turned a corner and there she was, taking a pile of bedding from a cupboard. What a stroke of luck! This suited my plan perfectly.

"Maggie!" I called. "Just the person I wanted to see! I wonder if you could do me an enormous favour?"

Maggie looked up, full of uncertainty. "If I – er – can, madam," she murmured.

"Do you keep spare staff uniforms in there?"

"Yes, it's the linen store."

"Could you possibly lend me a maid's uniform? You see, I'd like to play a little party trick!"

"Oh, I don't know about that, madam . . ."

"It'll be perfectly all right. You won't get into trouble; I'll see to that."

Finally I got Maggie to agree to hand over a suitably sized uniform. However, there was another obstacle. I had the uniform – but now I had to get into a certain guest's room!'

Cluedo NOTES

Can you guess which guest's room Mrs Peacock wanted to explore?

Minutes later I was up in my room and changing into the uniform. Though I say it myself, I looked rather fetching!

To complete my plan, I had to further ingratiate myself with Maggie. Poor girl; I'm sure she was becoming thoroughly tired of me!

I emerged from my room, hoping no guests would see me! Maggie was pushing a trolley loaded with fresh linen. I walked alongside her.

"When are you goin' to play your game or whatever it is, madam?" she asked.

"Oh, a little later, when everyone's in a really merry mood," I answered. "I want to keep out of the way for a while. You don't mind if I join you? Then no one will recognize me!"

Maggie looked totally bewildered but she agreed. I accompanied her in and out of rooms, standing around chatting while she went about her tasks. Something about each room told me that it wasn't the one I was seeking.

Then, when I was nearly despairing, we entered the right room: this was confirmed by a letter lying on the dressing-table. It was addressed to the person I believed was guilty of stealing my jewellery!

"Maggie, I feel a bit faint with all the excitement," I said. Actually, it was quite true! "You carry on with the rooms while I rest here. Don't worry, this room is occupied by a very old friend of mine. A party guest, in fact!"

Maggie obviously knew better than to argue, and as soon as she left the room, I set to work!

The dressing-table drawers revealed nothing – but a search of the wardrobe brought me the prize! A jewellery box, empty except for the bottom layer, which contained a sealed, padded envelope. I took a deep breath and tore it open. There inside was – my necklace!

"Stealing from guests, eh?" boomed a familiar voice from behind me. "I'll call the police . . .!"

I swung round and replied with a smile, "No, Lady Mulberry, it's *you* who must answer to *me* – for stealing my jewellery!"'

Everyone at the dinner-table gasped.

'Lady Mulberry!' whistled Mrs White.

'So that's why she's not been seen around the social circles of late,' sniffed Mustard.

'Yes,' said Mrs Peacock. 'She escaped prosecution by fleeing to her villa in Spain, where she still is. Her accomplice, however, didn't get off so lightly.'

*Cluedo*⁷ NOTES

Who was Lady Mulberry's accomplice?

'It was Sam, the assistant manager!' announced Mrs Peacock triumphantly. 'It seems he's a real expert at repairing – and faking – jewellery. He once worked for Formby & Metcalfe, but he made fake pieces and swapped them for real ones, which he sold. The fakes were so good, and the customers so trusting of such a reputable business, that he got away with it for some time. Then he was found out and quietly sacked to avoid scandal and loss of faith among the customers.

'For a while Lady Mulberry, who knew him from his Formby & Metcalfe days, employed him as an odd-job man, till he came to work here at the hotel. She collects diamonds like sweets, and she had her eye on mine, but she couldn't decide whether or not to buy them. When she did make up her mind, she was furious to be told by the assistant at Formby & Metcalfe that I'd bought them. She mentioned it to Sam, who confided in her that he had faked those pieces before he was sacked . . . so there we are!'

'How on earth did you work it all out?' asked Mrs White.

'I didn't know all the background till later, of course, but here's how I determined who the culprits were.

'It was when Lady Mulberry took her handkerchief from her evening bag. I noticed her elaborate watch and remembered her saying earlier that someone called Sam, who once worked at Formby & Metcalfe, had repaired it.

'Then I heard James call his assistant "Sam" – a "Sam" who had worked for a titled lady! I put two and two together. Lady Mulberry is almost as expert about jewellery as Mr Kingston ... that's why her jewellery box was empty. She wears it all at once, like a Christmas tree! If Lady Mulberry was innocent, she would have told me my jewels were fake. I could also see that her evening bag contained no jewellery, so I had to check the safe. Once I knew that it, too, was empty, I guessed they'd be in her room. It simply all added up!'

'And to think we were all there, yet never suspected a thing!' remarked Mustard. 'It certainly didn't spoil the party!'

'No, I like to think that Antonia's evening was a great success all round!' beamed Mrs Peacock.

Nothing to Declare

Blanche White decided it was time to tell her story. 'I got a tale about the sea!' she announced in a swashbuckling manner.

'Piracy?' asked Reverend Green.

'Not quite, but pretty bloodcurdlin' stuff, all the same!'

'I was on compassionate leave from my job here. Dr Black gave me a couple o' weeks off whilst I went to nurse my old Uncle Seth, who had sent word that 'e was ill with bronchitis. The poor ol' soul lived alone and he was terrified of 'ospitals, so I had no choice but to go an' 'elp out.

To tell you the truth, I was really lookin' forward to going back to Penrhuin, the charmin' little village on the Cornwall coast. It was a beautiful place in the warm summer sunshine; full of character, with lots of quaint, twisting streets an' colour-washed houses dotted around in no particular order.

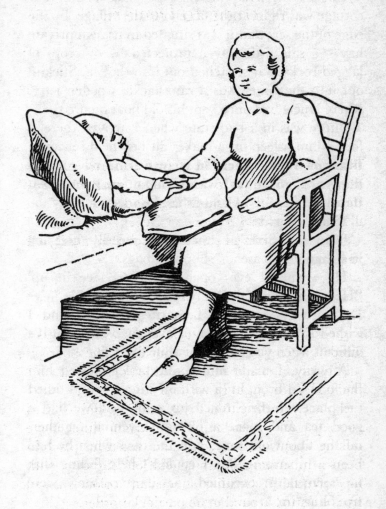

Uncle Seth lived in the best place of all. His cottage was right at the far end o' the village, by the edge of the sea; and it was situated in its own private bay – a safe little haven protected by outcrops of jagged rocks that stretched out into the sea. Stickin' out into the water was a ramshackle wooden jetty, where Uncle had once kept his old boat moored.

But 'e was in a bad state when I arrived there. I found him asleep on a makeshift bed he'd set up in the front room, where he kept warm and cosy by the hearth. Well, that was the intention, except that the grate was full of cold ashes; he was evidently too ill to light the fire.

"Mornin', Seth," I greeted 'im cheerily, breezing in with my suitcase an' shopping bags.

His wrinkled eyes opened and 'is face lit up. "Hello, Blanche! It's lovely to see you again!"

I'd always been his favourite, I knew. And I wished I'd seen more of him over the years. But it's difficult when you lead a busy life like I do.

Anyway, I made him comfortable, showed him the food I'd brought in with me, lit a fire and tidied the place. He brightened up a lot, and we had a good tea and spent a pleasant evening together, talking about old times and the days when he had been a fisherman. But I couldn't help feeling that he seemed preoccupied, as if something were troubling 'im.

"What's bothering you?" I asked him bluntly.

"Oh, somethin' and nothin'," he replied. "It's jus' that a fella called Trevelyan keeps botherin' me. Reckons as 'e's buying this cottage from the landlord . . . an' 'e wants me out."

"Does 'e now?" I exclaimed. "We'll see about that! You've got rights, y'know. You've lived 'ere all your life, man an' boy."

It was getting late. Uncle was tired, and so was I. After 'e drifted off to sleep I walked up the narrow, creaky staircase to the bedroom above. As I was puttin' my clothes in the wardrobe I 'eard the muffled sound of a powerful engine. Turning out the light, I peered through the tiny square window that looked out to sea. There was a good moon, so I could see quite well.

A big cabin-cruiser was coming, without any lights, into the bay. It slowed down and then manoeuvred expertly alongside the jetty. A couple of figures jumped down from the deck and tied up the vessel.

I didn't give the matter much thought as I settled down in the big, soft bed. Probably just some tired boat enthusiasts glad of somewhere to moor for the night, I thought. But all the same, it was funny they didn't have those little red and green lights that boats usually switch on at night . . .

"There was a boat by the jetty," I said at breakfast next morning. "But it was gone when I got up."

"Oh, I 'eard it. Probably anglers. Been comin' a couple o' times a week for the past month or so," answered Uncle Seth. "Does no 'arm, I suppose. Kind o' nice to think of a boat in the bay again!"

Suddenly there was terrible hammerin' at the front door!

"Customs and Excise! Open up, please!" shouted a deep, commanding voice.

I ran to the door an' swung it open. Without invitation, two burly, uniformed men strode into Uncle's front room.

"What's this?" he cried, sitting up in alarm.

"We're investigating reports of a cruiser without lights using this bay at night —"

"Ho! You think I'm a smuggler!" chuckled Uncle.

"That's what we're here to investigate," replied one of the customs officers sheepishly.

"Well, you go an' investigate all you like! Search my 'ouse if you want. But I guarantee you won't find anythin' out of order."

"Uncle Seth's not well, and I'm here to look after him," I explained.

"It looks as if we've made a mistake," said the officer humbly, glancing round at the simply furnished interior.

"You haven't altogether. There *is* a boat that

comes to the jetty. I saw it last night. But it's nothing to do with us."

The next couple o' days passed uneventfully. Uncle Seth's chest improved and he was able to potter around the cottage once again.

He continued to sleep downstairs whilst I occupied his bedroom. Then one night, feelin' uncomfortably hot, I sat on the edge of the bed and looked out to sea. The mystery boat was there again! A shiver of excitement ran down my spine and I made up my mind to take a closer look at it.

I donned my bright pink dressing-gown and crept silently out of the house and down to the jetty. Now I could see this wasn't the same boat I had seen a few nights before: it was considerably bigger. I read the name on its side: *La Mouette*. French for "Seagull", I thought; it was one of the few words I remembered from my schooldays!

From my vantage point – behind a small, tumbledown wooden tool-shed at the end o' the jetty – I saw three men, dressed in dark clothes, on board. They seemed totally preoccupied in doing some work on the front deck, so I crept on board at the stern and took a look round. There in the cockpit stood a wooden crate. Contraband, without a doubt! The top was loose, so I lifted it and peeked inside. To my disappointment, all it contained were a folding picnic-table, some chairs and a small paraffin stove – all well-used and hardly likely to bring a fortune on the black market!

The heavy lid slipped from my fingers and fell back down with a bang.

"What was that?" I heard a man exclaim.

I managed to dash back off the boat in the nick o' time and hid behind the tool-shed. The men scoured the boat in vain.

"Nothin' amiss," shouted one.

"OK, back to work, you vagabonds," ordered the leader. "We've got to buckle to if we're going to finish and get away before daybreak!"

Unfortunately I couldn't see what they were actually doin', except that I could smell fresh paint in the air. I was also stuck in my hiding-place because the leader remained in the stern, sitting idly with his legs dangling over the side, and he would have spotted me creeping back along the jetty. But I *did* manage to sneak into the shed, where I sat down – and eventually dozed off!

Vroom! The throbbin' o' powerful marine engines woke me with a start. Pushing the shed door slightly ajar and looking out cautiously, I saw the boat moving slowly away from the jetty and putting out to sea.

As I made my way leisurely back to the cottage, it came to me what these nautical types were up to. They were smugglers – of a sort!'

Cluedo NOTES

Can you work out what their game is? There are three clues which should have helped you.

'The mysterious night-time visitors to the bay weren't smuggling goods: it was the boats themselves that were the loot! That's why this was a different boat from the previous one I'd seen. That's why those men were working through the night – repainting the vessel. And that's why *La Mouette* now bore the name *Mystique*! They were stealing boats from France, sailing across the Channel to my uncle's secluded bay, renaming and painting them, and then presumably selling them to unsuspecting boat enthusiasts at knock-down prices!

The next day, Uncle Seth was feeling much stronger, so I suggested we take a walk down to the village. The hot afternoon sun made our stroll round the shops very pleasant. But we had a nasty surprise when we sat in Katy's Kitchen enjoying a pot of tea and some tasty scones with cream and jam.

"How very nice to see you out and about, Seth!" came an oily voice. A tall, slim man in a business suit joined us at our table.

"Oh, it's you, Trevelyan," groaned Uncle. "Now don't you go causin' any trouble with me or my niece!"

"Wouldn't dream of it, old boy," purred Trevelyan. "There's no reason why we can't remain the best of friends – so long as you buckle to and find somewhere else to live as quickly as possible!"

"Don't you speak to Uncle Seth like that!" I snapped. "'E's lived in that cottage all his life. You can't just throw 'im out, even if you're the landlord – which you're not!"

"Not yet, but I soon will be when the legal work's complete. I'm buying the property from Lord Cransfield, you see. And I'll be turfing you two vagabonds out on your ears! Good morning."

Trevelyan smiled sweetly at the other customers in the café as he rose from his seat and left.

"What's goin' to 'appen to me, Blanche?" Uncle was almost crying.

I threw back my head and laughed.

"Blanche – this is serious!" he implored me.

"Dear, dear Uncle Seth, nothing's going to happen to you! You won't lose your home – I'll see to that." I held his hands across the table. "Because I've realized something that signals a nasty end for Mr Trevelyan. Trust me!"'

Cluedo' NOTES

What has Mrs White noticed about Trevelyan?

'Trevelyan and the leader of the men on board the boat were one and the same person! In the café he had just used the same two unusual expressions – "buckle to" and "vagabonds" – that I had over-heard the previous night.

I left Uncle Seth with a second pot o' tea and went out to find a telephone box.

"Hello, Inquiries?" I said. "I'd like the telephone number o' the nearest HM Customs and Excise office, please . . ."

I was jumpy for the next three nights, for I was waitin' for the next night-time appearance of a boat in Uncle's bay. I woke at regular intervals to check through the bedroom window. And then, of course, a large cabin-cruiser turned up when I had lapsed and fallen into a deep sleep!

My watch said three a.m. so the boat 'ad probably been there for hours! From under my pillow I grabbed the two-way radio, given to me by a kind customs man who had responded to my telephone call by paying me a visit. My instructions were to call him up the moment I observed another sus-picious craft.

"Hello? Hello? Blanche W-White to Control!" I stammered nervously, pressing the little button. "Action stations down at the bay!"

"Roger. Message received and understood. Out," came the efficient reply.

I was annoyed with myself for having botched up the task. It was nearly light, so the stolen vessel would be miles away before the customs patrol boat arrived. Unless . . .

Still in my nightclothes and pink dressing-gown, I dashed down the jetty to the cruiser. With me I had the radio and a roll of sticky tape. I wrapped tape round and round the radio in order to keep the "transmit" button down. Then, seeing the three criminal crew members occupied, I took a chance and slipped on board. I was about to plant the radio in a locker near the control console, hoping that the customs men would be able to track the signal. But it was not to be: instead I was surprised by none other than Trevelyan.

"Ah! The old fool's niece is a stowaway!" he said coldly and calmly. "Lock her in the forward cabin, boys, until I decide what to do with her!"'

'We had been at sea for what seemed like hours. I sat glumly by the window in the cabin, awaiting my fate. Unknown to my captors I was able to maintain a whispered conversation over the radio with the customs men. But it wasn't much use, for I didn't know where I was. Until, that is, I heard one of the motley crew shout, "Poole Harbour ahead!"

I snatched the radio from my pocket and relayed this snatch of information.

"Right, Blanche, we'll have our men waiting at Poole," came the reply. "Any idea of the name or type of craft you're in?"

"Not a clue," I admitted, feeling stupid.

"It's such a busy spot, you see. It will be difficult for us to identify your boat."

"Yes," I hissed. "But there's nothing I can do. I'm still in my nightie and dressing-gown. Oh, wait a minute, there *is* something I can do!"'

Cluedo NOTES

How can Blanche White make identification clear to the harbour patrol?

"Blanche White to Control," I whispered. "Tell your local patrol that they must apprehend the vessel flyin' the Pink Dressing-Gown flag!"

I then removed my dressing-gown and pushed it outside, trapping the end in the window. It fluttered and flapped wonderfully in the breeze as we entered Poole Harbour, but it was too low down for Trevelyan or his men to see. Within minutes we were intercepted – and I was free again!'

'Goodness, what a story!' exclaimed Plum, sitting forward in his seat with excitement. 'So the baddies were carted off to prison?'

'That's right,' nodded Mrs White.

'And Uncle Seth?' asked Mrs Peacock.

'Uncle Seth's alive and well and still living in Penrhuin – an' Lord Cransfield says 'e can stay there for the rest of his days. 'E's been right as rain since I 'elped 'im. Gone and bought 'imself a little dinghy too! Must be my wonderful cookin'!'

An Heir Out of Place

'Dear me, I'm still wearing this ridiculous costume!' declared Colonel Mike Mustard, rising to his feet and wriggling out of the gorilla costume. 'I'd quite forgotten about it. No wonder I'm so hot.'

'Am I correct in assuming your tale takes place in the jungle?' asked Reverend Green.

'Nothing so exciting. The wilds of darkest Yorkshire.' Mustard finally managed to throw off the hairy suit, and sat down again. 'My crime story happened ten years or so ago . . .'

'It began with a call from my old army pal, Fred Bickerstaff. He farms several hundred acres in West Yorkshire. Likes the country life, y'know. Always been a bluff, no-nonsense type but when he rang me on this occasion, I could sense at once that old Fred wasn't quite himself. So I agreed to visit him the following weekend.

Going to bachelor Fred's place is rather a shock to the system – even for me. He lives way up on the moors, in a huge stone house. Fred doesn't believe in wasting money on modern gadgets and luxuries. Oh, no, it's basic amenities only. You have to be hardy to survive a stay there, I can tell you! The only concession he allows himself is a little help from Mrs Wagthorpe. She must be pushing eighty by now, but she's still there, cooking endless Yorkshire puddings and apple pies for Fred.

When I arrived, the autumn sky was darkening and the wind was blowing around those sturdy stone walls. Fred greeted me warmly, and Mrs Wagthorpe brought me a tea-tray complete with home-made scones and jam. Fred and I sat in the large drawing-room, with its bare floors, lofty ceiling and, thankfully, roaring log fire.

"Good to see you, my old friend!" said Fred. Then in typical Fred-style he came straight to the point. "To tell you the truth, Mike, I need a bit o' help and advice. It's about my great-nephew, Morgan. He's turned up sort of unexpected."

"Unexpectedly?"

"I'll say. I'd forgotten he existed!"

'That *is* unexpected!"

Fred explained more fully. "I did know he was

coming, because he wrote to me a few weeks ago.
But that was the first I'd heard of him for donkey's
years. He's my brother Jim's grandson. Jim once
sent me a photo of his daughter and grandchild, but
that was about it."

He continued; telling me about his brother, who
went out to Australia to farm sheep, and how over
the years they lost touch. Fred wasn't the sort to
spend money on airmail post or international telephone calls. Next thing he heard was that his brother
and sister-in-law had passed away.

As you'd expect, Fred, being so careful with his
pennies, had amassed a tidy fortune, which he
planned to leave to his particular friends, including
Mrs Wagthorpe's family, his favourite local charit-
ies, the church, and so on. Any possible family
claims he dismissed. As far as he was concerned,
there was no one. That is – until Morgan turned
up!

"Fact is, when I heard from the young feller, I
was over the moon," chuckled Fred. "I thought I'd
no relatives left. Call me an old fool if you like, but
I immediately changed my will in his favour."

I must admit I was surprised! It seemed out of
character for Fred, but it just goes to show how
pleased he must have been to hear from his family.

When Morgan arrived in person, he was young,
brash and not shy about stating that, as Fred's only

living relative, he would one day own this beautiful, windswept stretch of moorland!

But then Fred went on to tell me that he was convinced Morgan was an imposter! I laughed at first: he was simply being his usual, cautious self again. As I listened to him, however, I came to see that he was genuinely suspicious and concerned.

"I don't rightly know *why* the young feller's not Jim's daughter's lad. Suffice to say that I *do* know it! Funny thing is, he's brought a pile of old letters with him; letters I sent to Jim before we lost touch."

"Genuine?" I asked.

"Aye, they're genuine all right. Here's one."

Fred handed me a letter, folded in two, the edges yellowing with age. In it Fred had recalled childhood adventures he and Jim had enjoyed: "Remember how we used to spend days at Thickle Hollow during the summer? What grand times we had . . ."

"Thickle Hollow!" smiled Fred, his eyes sparkling at the recollection. "We *did* have grand times there! You had to be careful, mind. It's a cave in the hillside and it floods during heavy storms. A few people have drowned in there."

Suddenly a car screeched to a stop on the gravel drive outside the house.

"He's here," growled Fred, pushing the letter into his waistcoat-pocket. "Say nowt about about what I've told you, but take notice and see what you think of the cheeky so-and-so."

Morgan was certainly full of bounce and confidence. He was a good-looking chap with fair hair, blue eyes and a sunny complexion.

"Nice to meet a mate of Uncle Fred's!" he drawled with a huge grin, shaking my hand vigorously. He lay back on the sofa, placing his feet upon the coffee-table. His manner was casual and relaxed, and seemed a touch arrogant to an old trooper like me.

I asked about his life in Australia and which part he came from.

"Way out in the west. Sheep-farming country. A great life, mate! It's a marvellous place! What with the Barrier Reef and everything! I tell you, there are sharks and fishes you've never seen before. It's incredible. I've never been anywhere but Oz before . . . but now," he stretched out his arms lazily, "this is my future abode!"

"Have you lost both parents?" I asked, trying to sound politely interested.

"Yeah, unfortunately. Both eaten by crocs in the Blue Ridge Mountains – right on our doorstep, too."

I'll spare you the gory account of their demise. But as I lay in bed that night, listening to the howling wind, I came round to Fred's way of thinking, that our young visitor was indeed an imposter!'

Cluedo NOTES

What led Colonel Mustard to agree with Fred that Morgan was faking?

'Geography has never been my strong point but I was sure that the Blue Ridge Mountains weren't in Western Australia – they were in Virginia, USA! And they certainly weren't crocodile territory! A quick check in Fred's atlas next morning confirmed I was right.

We enjoyed an enormous breakfast, cooked and served by the admirable Mrs Wagthorpe. Fred was quiet, obviously deep in thought, but Morgan chattered away. He told us how he'd decided to look up his old Uncle Fred on the advice of his lawyer in Australia. He'd arrived in England only the week before and had stayed in London for a few days' sightseeing, before hiring a car and driving up to Yorkshire.

We were still there when Mrs Wagthorpe announced she was going into the village to do some shopping.

"Don't forget to bring me a packet of chocolate biscuits, Mrs Wagthorpe," called Morgan.

"I won't forget, Mr Morgan," beamed the kindly old lady, clearly charmed by the young schemer.

"Wasting good brass on fancy stuff," grumbled Fred. "What's wrong with Mrs Wagthorpe's home-baked scones?"

"Nothing at all, Uncle," replied Morgan. "They're the best scones I've tasted outside Scotland. It's simply that I'm partial to chocolate bickies as well."

I took a stroll in the grounds. The wind was still strong, and dark clouds could be seen over the moor. Questions needed to be addressed. Morgan's motive was clear enough: to get his hands on Fred's land and fortune. But how did he find out about it? How did he come to have genuine letters from Fred to Jim? Where was the real Morgan? Or were we falsely accusing the fellow?

"I'm sure feeling the cold!" came a voice from behind.

Turning round, I found Morgan standing beside me.

'It's always been the sunshine for me," he continued in his Australian accent.

"Mmm, I daresay," I replied rather vacantly, because Morgan's hired car had taken my attention.

It was smart and gleaming, a new model I'd read about in the press but not actually seen before.

"Superb car," I said. "May I sit inside and try her for size?"

"Sure you can."

Morgan opened the driver's door and I slid on to the soft leather seat and waggled the gears. It had the distinctive, exciting smell of a new car and the mileometer showed ninety-five miles. On the passenger seat lay an Australian newspaper.

"Storm's still brewing," said Morgan. "Happen

BRIGGLES GARAGE of LEEDS

I'll take a drive through the countryside before it starts pouring down."

I left the car and he took over, driving off at high speed.

Good! I thought. This gave me an opportunity to investigate without arousing his suspicions.

I asked Fred to show me the old photograph of

Morgan and his parents. It showed a happy young couple sitting on a beach with a little boy. The child had a mop of dark curly hair and huge blue eyes.

"He doesn't look a bit like the baby in the photograph," I observed.

"Aye!" Fred's big face beamed, then clouded slightly. "But that's not proof, is it? He's just a nipper in the picture, and kids change as they grow, don't they?"

"Yes, but not in that way. Lots of babies have fair hair that darkens as they age, but not usually the other way round."

"He could have dyed it." Fred wrinkled his nose in disgust.

"I hardly think the matter needs considering," I said gravely. "I'm now certain that our friend is an imposter. And that's not all . . . I believe he's as much of a Yorkshireman as you are!" '

Cluedo NOTES

Since the last CLUEDO NOTES Mustard has spotted four more little clues which have given 'Morgan' away. What are they?

1.

2.

3.

4.

'"Your house guest has tripped himself up in several ways," I revealed. "Firstly, he reckoned he'd never been out of Australia before, yet he declared Mrs Wagthorpe's scones to be the best he'd tasted outside Scotland."

"You're right!"

"Secondly, there's his hired car. It's from a firm in Leeds. The sticker in the back window says so."

"Well?"

"If he'd hired it in London, as he said, it would hardly be from a Leeds garage. And, thirdly, with only ninety-five miles on the clock, it cannot possibly have been anywhere near London!"

Fred slapped his thigh in delight. "You're a sharp 'un, Mike! But I don't think you're right about him being from Yorkshire. He's the funniest sounding Yorkshireman I've ever heard, and I'm one, born and bred!"

"Fourthly," I replied with satisfaction, "Morgan said to me just now, 'Happen I'll take a drive through the countryside . . .' Sounds more like Wakefield than Woomera to me!"

"Bah! I wish I could meet Jim's real grandson," murmured Fred wistfully.

With a bit of luck, you *may*, I thought, wondering where his genuine great-nephew was at this moment. What to do next? Confront the imposter when he returned? But what if he simply fled, leaving no further clues as to the whereabouts of the real Morgan? No, I had to solve the mystery without arousing suspicion.

"Is there a telephone number on the letter Morgan sent you initially?" I asked.

Fred nodded and fished the letter from his pocket.

"Mind if I ring Australia?"

"Not if it'll help."

I called the number shown on the letter. A woman answered. I asked for Morgan and she replied that this was the number of his apartment, that she was his cleaner and that he'd left some three weeks earlier to visit his uncle in England.

"Just as I thought. Your nephew *is* over here," I told Fred.

Swift action was needed now, I decided, making my way up the stairs to Morgan's room. Luckily there was no lock on the door. I can't say I liked sneaking around someone else's personal possessions, but these were special circumstances.

Unfortunately, one of the dressing-table drawers was locked. I imagined it contained the imposter's passport and other documents that might have given him away. On the bedside table was a book about Yorkshire caves, and a muddle of assorted pens and keys. Opening the wardrobe revealed an untidy pile of clothes. Shoes and magazines tumbled out. Some things were stuffed into plastic bags. As I struggled to shove everything back inside, something very strange fell from a brown sack. It was a heap of unopened post: envelopes of all shapes and sizes, some opened, some not.

This was a totally unexpected find! In amazement I sat on the floor and examined the letters. They were all addressed to local people and businesses and bore postmarks more or less the same date. A label on the sack showed that it had come from Bridgeforge sorting-office.

A car drew up outside. Morgan was back! Frantically I searched for the letter I hoped would be there. Yes, it was! I pushed it into my pocket, closed the wardrobe door and returned downstairs.

The time had come to do some investigations in Bridgeforge, the nearest small town. I greeted Morgan stiffly as I passed him in the porch.

"Messy on those moors," he said awkwardly, struggling out a pair of mud-caked wellingtons.

Once in Bridgeforge, I bought a cup of tea in a cafe and sat down to study the letter from Morgan's wardrobe. It was from the *real* Morgan to Fred, posted from Australia and giving the time and place of his arrival in London. 'I'll stay in London for a few days, then catch the train to see you . . .'

By train! This was great stuff! The nearest railway station to Fred's was right here in Bridgeforge! I'd call there later, but first I had somewhere else to go.

The Post Office was just around the corner. I explained that I'd seen letters lying about in a pile of rubbish, which was quite true! One of the staff remembered the missing post at once.

"Some mail went missing from this office," he admitted. "But it wasn't our staff to blame. We had decorators in that day, and I suspect it was a particular young chap, because the following day he disappeared and his boss didn't know where he'd gone. The police couldn't find him either."

"Do you know his name?"

"Sorry, can't recall it. There's no proof, mind."

"I realize that. I'll inform the police about my find."

I intended to do just that – but not quite yet. My next area of investigation was the railway station. I asked the station master if he recalled seeing a young Australian getting off the train in the past week or so.

He rubbed his chin thoughtfully. "Sarah might know. She's a grand memory for folk who aren't local."

Sarah, the ticket collector, *did* remember him! "Yes, a dark young man with an Australian accent. His friend picked him up in a car and they drove off Thickle way."

"Is that anywhere near Fred Bickerstaff's place?"

"Oh, no, in the completely opposite direction."

"What was his friend like?"

"I can tell you *who* he was! Tony Smethers. He was at school with my kids. Never liked him, though. He was a very sly child."

What a stroke of luck! Things were beginning to fall into place now – and I had a hunch where I might find the real Morgan.'

Cluedo® NOTES

Where does Mustard think he is?

'I guessed that the real Australian relative was being kept in Thickle Hollow! The Yorkshire caves book on the bedside table . . . the muddy wellingtons . . . the ticket collector's report that the two men had gone off towards Thickle instead of Fred's house . . . the evidence was too much to ignore.

The sky was almost black, and I remembered that Thickle Hollow flooded in storms. It was now going to be a race against time! I summoned the help of the local police constable. We picked up two local rescue volunteers and drove over to Thickle Moor.

Lightning flashed and thunder crashed, and heavy rain lashed against us as we stumbled across the rough terrain to the mouth of the notorious cave. The rescue-men led the way inside with powerful torches. We went deeper and deeper, along a narrow passage that became narrower and lower all the time.

Eventually we squeezed through an uncomfortably small gap and found ourselves in a spacious cavern. I was right! There, in front of our eyes, sat a bedraggled young man, bound hand and foot, his dark eyes ablaze with fear.

"Let's get him out of here before it floods!" cried one of the rescue-men.

"Th-thanks," was all Morgan could mutter.

How relieved we all were! And what a great party

we had a couple of days later at Fred's! Why, that dour old house had never seen anything like it! Fred was overjoyed at finding his great-nephew, especially as he very nearly ended up leaving his fortune to the scoundrel Tony Smethers!'

'**So this Smethers character had stolen the mail, read Morgan's letter and realized this was an opportunity to make his fortune, eh?' asked Mrs Peacock.**

'Exactly,' replied Mustard. 'He was an opportunist criminal. Whilst working as a decorator he took a chance and stole a sack of mail. From the letter, it was clear that Fred and his great-nephew had never met. So he met him at the station, pretending to be a friend of Fred's, and took the unsuspecting fellow to Thickle Hollow. He overpowered him, forced him into the cave and kept him bound and fed there, in case he needed to extract any information from him. But, being local, he knew quite well that the place would flood eventually – a most convenient way to dispose of his victim!'

'Villainous!' snorted Plum.

'You should have seen his face when we walked into Fred's house with Morgan. The coward ran upstairs and hid under the bed.

Fred had to poke him out with his shepherd's crook!' laughed Mustard.

'Where is he now?' queried Vivienne.

'Languishing in gaol – whilst the real Morgan has brought new life and laughter into old Fred's life. His parents had, sadly, died; not eaten by crocs, but in a car accident. But old Fred and Morgan get on like a house on fire. So really it's a story with a very happy ending!'

Wakey, Wakey, Rise and Shine

'I think you'll be rather surprised when I reveal the location of my mystery,' smiled Reverend Jonathan Green. 'Sandy Bay Holiday Camp at Sandytown-on-Sea.'

'That's very popular,' commented Mrs White.

'It is now,' agreed Reverend Green, 'but just a couple of years ago it was in grave danger of closure.'

'Really?' exclaimed Vivienne. 'Whenever I drive past the place these days, it seems to be thriving. Not my idea of the perfect holiday, of course.'

'Nor mine,' said Reverend Green. 'But, you see, my cousin, Henry Murgatroyd owns the place. He's from the flamboyant side of the family, may I add!'

'When he rang me, he was in a terrible state. The tale he told me seemed quite extraordinary and I wondered if he was exaggerating. His camp was being sabotaged, he said! Everything was going disastrously wrong and the campers were furious! The swimming pool had mysteriously drained overnight, the brakes kept failing on the little train that took the children around the camp, the food tasted horrible, the chalets were insect-infested, entertainers didn't turn up for shows . . . and they were just a few examples! If things didn't improve, he'd have to sell up at a loss or go bankrupt.

Naturally I offered to come down and help, although, to be honest, I couldn't see how I could possibly do much.

When I arrived at Sandy Bay, Henry told me his plan! "I want you to be a 'mole'!" he said.

"A mole?"

"That's right! I've tried every way I can think of to find out what's at the bottom of all this, but I've got nowhere. Then I had this brilliant idea! You must join the camp entertainment team and see if you can do any better!"

"What, me?" I asked, incredulously.

"Of course! Your magic act will go down a treat!"

I do a few tricks for the children's Christmas parties in the village hall, you see, but to entertain hundreds of people on a professional basis – that was quite different. However, despite my objections, Henry managed to persuade me. His suspicions were centred upon Jeremy, the Entertainments Manager. He didn't have any proof, but he just thought Jeremy seemed a sly and slimy character.

"In fact, I rather wish I hadn't taken him on," Henry confessed. "But I was desperate at the time. My former Entertainments Manager was about to retire."

I felt silly, being introduced to Jeremy as "Mr Amazo" the magician, though I must admit that the idea of working as a kind of undercover agent was rather exciting.

"I'd like you to give him a try," Henry told Jeremy.

"Great!" was Jeremy's comment. "We're in dire need of a good magic act. The kids love it! What's your real name, by the way?"

"Jonathan Green," I replied truthfully.

"OK, Jonathan. Start this afternoon. Kids' concert, four thirty sharp. We'll see how you shape up. Who knows, you might become a permanent member of the entertainments team!"

Before I settled into my chalet – quite cosy it was too, by the way – I took a stroll around the camp, accompanied by Aunty Jill, a leading Orange Coat and clearly very popular with everyone!

"You'll love it here, Jonathan," she said brightly, in between calling out greetings to numerous children. "We'd be having a great season if it weren't for this trouble. The police can't seem to do anything. No one sees anything. There's no way of knowing when or where they'll strike next. This morning, lots of campers found that their car tyres had been let down."

"A terrible problem," I agreed. "We must all keep a lookout!"

"Oh, let me introduce you to Bob! We're Aunty Jill and Uncle Bob to the kids!"

"Pleased to meet you!" said Bob, shaking hands with me. "Hope you'll be happy here, despite what's going on!"

As I got ready for the concert, I thought about my task. At present, there seemed to be no clues whatsoever. But, since arriving at the camp, I'd become determined to find out who was behind the horrid activities. It was such a shame for the families, who deserved a happy holiday, not an ordeal.

By the end of the childrens' concert I was exhausted ... but exhilarated too! Pulling rabbits – fluffy toy ones! – out of hats and making objects disappear with a wave of my magic wand could be hard work, especially when one is surrounded by a horde of yelling, excited boys and girls. But it was terrific fun and I was really looking forward to my

evening appearance at the camp's cabaret theatre.

This was an altogether different affair, with mums and dads, plus some older children. I decided to try my lie-detector test! This is a little contraption I invented when I was a very young man. I used to amuse my family and friends with it no end! It's not a proper piece of equipment, of course, but it can sometimes work, after a fashion.

Briefly, what happens is that I ask a volunteer to put his or her hand on a plastic panel. If the hand is very moist, a red bulb lights up and a bell sounds. The theory is that if someone isn't telling the truth, the hand will be sweaty! Some performances could be quite embarrassing, as, if I was performing in very warm conditions, everyone would appear to be a liar, whereas on a chill winter evening in our draughty village hall, simply all the population seemed incapable of telling a lie!

Jill, dressed up in a glamorous outfit, introduced me as Mr Amazo, and I received a warm welcome from the audience.

"Good evening, everyone!" I said. "Are you all having a wonderful holiday?"

I immediately wished I hadn't asked that, because, although many replied with a resounding "Yes", there were also some definite grumblings of discontentent.

Swiftly I passed on to my lie-detecting trick, inviting members of the audience to take part.

"Jill will show you what to do!" I said.

Within seconds, an eager line of assorted volunteers had lined up on the stage, all standing giggling in front of my lie-detector. I explained how it worked and then asked Jill to be the first participant. She smiled broadly as I asked the first question.

"Make sure you keep your hands on the plastic panel while you answer the question," I reminded her. "Now, your full name is Jill White, isn't it?"

"Yes, that's the truth," answered Jill with a sudden frown as the red light flashed and the bell rang.

"Well, really!" I laughed. "My machine informs me you're telling a fib! Are you deceiving us, Jill – or could it be Jenny?"

"Your stupid machine doesn't work!" hissed Jill. "Please, Jonathan, I feel such a fool!"

At that moment, I felt such a fool too. Even under the heavy make-up Jill's blushing was clear to see. Why should she be so put-out, I wondered? Unless ... unless she was hiding something. I quickly carried on with the next volunteer.

Next day dawned bright and sunny. Perfect for the camp sporting events. Along with the rest of the entertainment team, I was down on the playing field, organizing Five-a-Side football matches, netball games, cricket, running and lots more. In overall charge of campers' sport was a bluff, cheery chap called Rodney. My cousin Henry seemed pleased to have him on the staff.

"We've got to push sport," Henry said. "It's the thing these days. All the big, famous camps employ professional sportspeople and even Shingle Bay camp, just along the coast, is owned by Rick Birstead, a former tennis player. We're lucky to have Rodney as sports manager. He's getting on a bit, but he's got useful contacts. He used to be a football reporter."

I joined Rodney in keeping scores. "I believe you were a football reporter," I said. "Must have been very interesting."

"Fascinating life, my dear chap!" he replied.

"What was the most exciting match you covered?" I asked.

"Mmm, er ... oh yes, of course! It has to be when England beat Italy at the Oval a few years back."

At last the sports events were over and I trudged gratefully towards my chalet to recover before the afternoon show. Henry caught up with me.

"Found anything out, Jonathan?" he asked.

"I don't know if this is anything to do with the trouble," I told him, "but I'm convinced your precious Rodney is lying about his past!"'

Cluedo NOTES

Why does Reverend Green think Rodney is lying?

'Henry looked at me aghast. "Why do you say that?"

"Well, Henry, I'm no football fan, but even I know that the Oval is a cricket ground."

"Of course!" exclaimed Henry. "Everyone knows that."

"Rodney doesn't. He said England and Italy played football there!"

Henry looked thoughtful. "So he might be involved in trying to ruin me. I knew from the start this was an inside job. But why?"

"We'll find out, never fear. Meantime, I must get out of this muddy track suit, and have a rest before facing my next audience!"

Despite my tiredness, I enjoyed that afternoon's show with the children. I was beginning to get a taste for show business! It gets in your blood, you know! I would have enjoyed the show even more, but for one curious thing. Just before I went on stage, Uncle Bob popped into the dressing room.

"Excuse me, I've come to collect a script," he said, leaning over me to reach a shelf. When I was almost ready to go on stage, I began to sneeze, violently. And I continued sneezing, on and off, throughout my performance. Luckily, I managed to turn my affliction into a running – or rather sneezing – joke and nobody minded. I told the audience that if I sneezed once more, they could put me in my own magic cabinet and make me disappear! Everyone laughed at that!

Later, I was feeling quite peckish as I made my way to the dining hall for my evening meal. The sea air and the day's energetic activities had sharpened my appetite. Aunty Jill walked up beside me.

"I'm sorry about last night," she said. "You see, Jill White is my stage name. I'm really called Edna Smith."

"Oh, it's all right," I answered, not knowing what to believe.

Was Jill – or Edna – involved in the sabotage of the camp? Before I could decide, we'd arrived at the dining hall.

"What's on the menu, Mabel?" I asked the waitress.

"Nothing, Jonathan," she gasped. "At least, nothing worth eating! The dinner's ruined – again! Third time this week! It's so peppery, no one can eat it. Everyone's up in arms!"

"How dreadful!" cried Jill, but she didn't sound very sincere to me.

There was nothing else for it but to venture outside the camp to a nearby fish and chip shop. Judging by the length of the queue, most of the campers had the same idea.

"My tongue's on fire!" grumbled one disgruntled woman.

"I want my money back!" a red-faced man said angrily. "Fancy lacing the food with tons of pepper!"

Suddenly, I felt a sneeze rising up in my nostrils. Fact was, I hadn't altogether stopped sneezing since ... since. That was it! I knew who had put pepper in the food!'

Cluedo? NOTES

Who do you think was responsible for 'hotting up' the dinner?

'I reported my discovery to Henry, but he didn't seem impressed.

"Bob? But he's our good old Uncle Bob! He's been with us for ten seasons . . . one of most loyal team members. Why would he do such a thing?"

"I don't know, Henry. But I aim to find out."

"Haven't you got anything on slimy Jeremy?"

"No, not yet. Oh dear, it's nearly time for my evening show!"

Camp entertainers certainly worked at a breathless pace! I decided to try another trick I'd been busily rehearsing. I just hoped it would work!

Wandering around the front of the audience, I picked a random assortment of people and invited them to come up on stage. One or two protested mildly, but good naturedly agreed in the end. The trick involved my asking the volunteers for small personal objects, which later reappeared in the magic cabinet or in my pocket. You know the kind of thing.

Each person handed me something. Keys, watches, wallets and so on. One young man handed me a bunch of several keys. A few minutes later, after I'd "found" these keys under my magician's hat, I was handing them back to their owner, when I noticed the name engraved on a large, brass key holder: "Shingle Bay Holiday Camp". It struck me as rather strange, considering that we were actually at Sandy Bay Camp.

I would have dismissed the matter, but for the young man's reaction. His face went bright red when he saw me staring at him. As he disappeared back into the audience, I decided to play a hunch.

"Close the theatre doors at once!" I called over the microphone. "The saboteur is in here. Don't let him escape!"

I'll never know how I had the presence of mind to make that announcement. It goes to show how quickly one can act in an emergency!

Henry turned up minutes later and I told him what had happened.

"This Rick person has obviously had his own little team right here, doing all the damage they could! Before we go after the others, let's find this bogus camper. He must still be in the theatre."

But he wasn't! At least, it seemed he wasn't. We looked everywhere, and the campers helped too.

"He's definitely not down here," called someone. "Are you sure he's not on the stage?"

"No," I answered, looking around. The stage was empty, except for my magic props. Then, suddenly, I realized where the culprit might be.'

Cluedo' NOTES

Where on the stage do you think the man is hiding?

'Very gingerly, I opened my magic cabinet. I was right! There, cringing inside, was the young man. He crept out and then seemed only too relieved to tell all!

Sure enough, Rick Birstead, owner of the rival camp, Shingle Bay, was behind it all! He was jealous about the rising popularity of Henry's camp and had set upon an evil plan to wreck it. He'd planted bogus campers to do the dreadful deeds and had also bribed the once-loyal Uncle Bob, with promises of a top job at Shingle Bay. As for Rodney, the so-called sports expert, he was none other than Rick's brother. That explained why he knew so little about football. Tennis was the Birstead forte!'

'So Jeremy, the Entertainments Manager, was innocent!' said Vivienne.

'Yes, and so was Jill – I mean Edna!' replied Reverend Green. 'And Henry's camp has gone from strength to strength! As for Shingle Bay, it closed down when Rick Birstead went to gaol, but Henry is now almost in a position to buy it for himself. As a magician might say, the tables have turned very nicely!'

Homeward Bound

The hour was late. The meal and the story-telling were over. Buccaneering Blanche, and her curiously dressed bunch of guests, wandered into the Library and draped themselves in chairs for a final few words before they left. It would be another year before they would all be together again.

Raymond, the hired butler, came in with a trayful of cups and a large pot of steaming coffee. He set it down on the table and made for the door.

'Oh, Raymond, may I have a quick word with you?' Vivienne Scarlett jumped up and followed him out of the room.

'Help yourself to coffee, everyone,' announced Mrs White, removing her eye-patch.

'Thank you all for tonight's enthralling stories,' added Mrs Peacock, 'and thank you for coming in such lovely costumes. Dr Black would have loved it if he'd been here.'

A few minutes later Vivienne slipped back into

the room and poured herself a warming drink; her bare arms were goose-pimpled with the cold.

Reverend Green came across to her. 'Care for a walk by the river, my dear?'

'What?'

'A walk by the river – *your* river!' Green raised his eyes in mock disappointment at the failure of his quip. 'It's a joke, Vivienne. You're Queen of the Nile – *River* Nile. Get it? I wish I hadn't bothered!'

'Oh, sorry to be slow on the uptake, Jonathan. I'm tired,' yawned Vivienne.

Shortly afterwards the sound of a large car could be heard pulling up on the crunchy gravel of the drive.

'That'll be my car,' declared Vivienne.

The imminent departure of Miss Scarlett stirred the rest of the guests into action. They left the Library and stood in the Hall, saying their goodbyes to Mrs Peacock, Mrs White and Raymond. Colonel Mustard stood on the step by the open front door. He looked out and gave a shout of surprise. 'Hey! My car's gone!'

'That's all right, Colonel,' said Raymond soothingly. 'The gorilla drove off in it!'

'Gorilla? Oh, David, you mean, earlier on.'

'No, sir. This was a much better-looking gorilla; more like yourself in appearance – when you're in costume, I mean.'

The guests giggled.

'B-but . . . Who? What . . .?' spluttered Mustard.

'I naturally assumed everything would be in order, sir. I presumed the gorilla had some connection with you.'

Then the front lamp of a bicycle flickered along the drive and up rode a village constable.

'Evenin' all!' he said, parking his machine and kicking down its little stand. 'I'm 'ere to warn you to watch out for a gorilla which has escaped from the local zoo –'

Mustard's face went purple. 'My beautiful sports car! D'you mean to tell me it's being driven by –'

'Calm down, sir. Now what appears to be the trouble?'

'My car's been stolen!'

'By the gorilla?'

'Yes!'

The officer placed his hands on his hips and drew a deep breath. 'I do 'ope you're not trying to make fun of me!'

'I'm *not*! You must get my car back, officer! I've spent years cherishing it.'

'I see, sir. Well, if you insist on continuing with your incredible claim, I'm afraid I must ask you to accompany me . . . in a little dance!'

With that the policeman produced a mouth-organ from his pocket and proceeded to play a merry tune whilst skipping about zanily.

Vivienne burst out laughing. 'Oh, Mike, you should see your face! This is Peter, your nephew David's partner, in his novelty greetings firm. I arranged all this whilst you were in the Library!'

The fake policeman bowed deeply. 'Your vehicle's quite safe, sir, round the side of the house. But in future please make sure your insurance policy covers drivers with big hairy hands!'

Everyone else laughed, and then so did Mustard.

The guests, and the hired butler and cook, had gone, and once again the big house fell silent. Without the late Dr Black, and the convivial company he used to invite regularly for dinner and parties, it was a sad and gloomy place. Except, that is, whenever Mrs Blanche White and Mrs Elizabeth Peacock invited Reverend Jonathan Green, Vivienne Scarlett, Professor Peter Plum and Colonel Mike Mustard to a get-together in memory of Dr Black.

Mrs White discarded her fancy-dress costume, visited the bathroom to wash briefly and brush her teeth, slipped into bed and pulled her sheets and blankets round her cosily. Then she reached out and switched off the lamp.

For a few moments she gazed up at the ornately plastered ceiling, barely discernible in the half-light. She smiled as she thought about the happy evening she had just spent. For a few minutes she thought of the next dinner-party and how she would organize it. Then she pondered the question of whether the police would ever apprehend the murderer of poor Dr Black. Gradually she drifted off to sleep; and then she was Buccaneering Blanche once again, enjoying a few sweet hours of exotic adventure on the high seas.